P9-BZA-309

To my two children,
Luke and Hayley
—P. K.
To Raechele and Jim
—J. C.

SIMON & SCHUSTER BOOKS FOR YOUNG READERS
An imprint of Simon & Schuster Children's Publishing Division
1230 Avenue of the Americas, New York, New York 10020
Text copyright © 2002 by Peter Kavanagh
Illustrations copyright © 2002 by Jane Chapman
First published as *Love Like This* in Great Britain in 2002 by
Little Tiger Press
First U.S. edition, 2003
All rights reserved, including the right of reproduction
in whole or in part in any form.
SIMON & SCHUSTER BOOKS FOR YOUNG READERS
is a trademark of Simon & Schuster.
Book design by Dan Potash
The text for this book is set in Meridien Roman.
Printed in Mexico
10 9 8 7 6 5 4 3 2 1
CIP data for this book is available from the Library of Congress.
ISBN 0-689-85691-1

Peter Kavanagh
Illustrated by Jane Chapman

I
Love
My
Mama

SIMON & SCHUSTER BOOKS FOR YOUNG READERS
New York • London • Toronto • Sydney • Singapore

The pale sun rises through the morning mist.
I love my mama on days like this.

When storm winds blow, we
shelter together. Nothing can harm
us while we have each other.

Later we chase across hot dusty plains, stomping and stamping and playing new games.

When the bright sun rises
hotter and higher, we stride along
by the cool fast river.

The water is clean and we're covered in dust. We jump in together and let it wash over us.

We dip and dive and splash and splish.
Fun like this is all we could wish.

We walk in the grass to dry in the sun
and sing together in trumpeting fun.

Sometimes we laugh for no reason at all,
comparing our trunks, one big, one small.

We gaze at the birds flying into the night
and the stars in the sky, all twinkly and bright.

And when we lie in the soft dewy grass,
you tell me elephant tales from the past.

Last thing at night we curl in a hug,
safe and happy, cozy and snug.

And we sink into sleep and dream of new days.

My mama's love surrounds me always.